Beware of the Cheese Princess

Charlie Bacon

Beware of the Cheese Princess

by Gary Hogg

ILLUSTRATED BY ELISE SUMMERS

Little Buckaroo Books

Text copyright © 2014 by Gary Hogg
Illustrations copyright © by Elise Summers
Designed by Matt Shay
ISBN 978-1-930771-138-6

Printed in the U.S.A.

10 9 8 7 6 5 4 3 2 1

For my dad,

Best of the Best.

Contents

Chapter 1
Where's Boogie?

"Charlie Bacon, you're late!" shouted his big sister, Shrudi. "School starts in twenty minutes."

Charlie's eyes blinked open. "Why didn't you wake me up?" he grumbled.

"I just did," said Shrudi. "Dad's already gone to school. You can have cereal for breakfast."

Charlie hopped out of bed and started digging through the pile of dirty clothes on the floor. "When's Mom coming back?" he asked.

"As soon as Grandma is feeling better," said Shrudi. "We should give her a big surprise when she gets home."

"I think the messy house will be surprise enough," said Charlie, pulling on a pair of dirty jeans. He hurried into the kitchen and grabbed the box of cereal.

"The bowls and spoons are all dirty," complained Charlie as he looked at the sink heaped with dirty dishes. He grabbed a mug from the cupboard and filled it with cereal. He opened the fridge and stared at the empty milk jug.

Charlie poured orange juice over his cereal. He pulled a huge serving spoon from the silverware drawer and dug in. He wolfed down the juicy cereal in record time and raced to the bathroom to brush his teeth.

Shrudi was in front of the mirror fussing with her hair. Charlie squirmed past her and grabbed the toothpaste and his toothbrush. He gave the toothpaste tube a tight squeeze at the exact moment his sister gave him a shove. A glob of minty toothpaste shot past his toothbrush and plastered the front of his shirt.

Charlie scraped the toothpaste off his shirt with his toothbrush and began brushing his teeth. His mouth was full of suds when Shrudi gave him a second shove. A spray of toothpaste and spit erupted from Charlie's mouth and sprayed the mirror.

"You better clean that up," said Shrudi as she left the room. Charlie rinsed his mouth and rubbed the mirror with the washcloth. He looked at the toothpaste smear across the front of his shirt and decided to turn the shirt inside out. He put on his shoes, grabbed his backpack, and dashed out the front door. Shrudi locked the door and followed him out.

Charlie raced down the street to Central Elementary. The morning bell was ringing as he hurried through the front door. He sped down the hall and made a quick detour into the cafeteria.

"Hi, Dad," shouted Charlie. Charlie's dad was the school's cook. Chef Jeff's face brightened into a smile when he saw his oldest son.

"Go get 'em, Charlie," he called out.

Charlie zoomed out the other side of the lunchroom and popped into Room 7. He set his backpack down and plopped into his seat. As he was trying to catch his breath, he noticed that everyone was staring at a red-haired lady who was sitting at Mr. Beecher's desk.

"Are you Mr. Beecher's wife?" asked Charlie's best friend, Biff. The lady grinned and replied, "No, I'm the substitute. Your teacher's on paternity leave for a few weeks."

"What's paternity leave?" asked Tyler.

"After having a baby, a parent can have some time

off work to be with the new child," explained the substitute.

"I didn't even know he was pregnant," said Biff.

The class laughed and the substitute cleared her throat. "Mr. Beecher's wife gave birth to a healthy baby boy yesterday."

The students burst into applause. Everyone was still talking about the big news when the substitute wrote her name on the smart board. "I'm Ms. Phillips and I'll be your teacher until Mr. Beecher returns," she explained.

Her introduction was interrupted by Dr. Brown's voice over the intercom as he read morning announcements. When the class stood to recite the Pledge of Allegiance, Charlie put his hand over his heart and said, "Where's Boogie?"

Chapter 2
Get That Lizard!

The entire class turned and stared at the terrarium. Ms. Phillips tried to get the class focused on reciting the pledge, but they paid no attention to her.

"He's probably hiding behind the rock," said Rayce. "He likes it there."

Charlie hurried over to the terrarium. "He's not here," he said. "Someone left the top open." The students began searching the room.

"Get back in your seats," demanded Ms. Phillips, but no one listened. They started tearing Room 7 apart in their search.

"We've got to find him," cried Shelby.

"He'll never survive on his own," added Allison.

"Stop!" yelled Ms. Phillips. The students froze and looked at the frustrated substitute teacher. "Who or what is Boogie?"

"Boogie is the coolest lizard on the face of the planet," said Biff. "He's going to win the Classiest Pet Contest for us."

"The what?" asked Ms. Phillips.

Allison explained, "Every year Central Elementary has a classroom pet contest. There's a special assembly where all the classes that have pets bring them to the multipurpose room. Someone from the class gives a report about their class pet. The winning class gets a trophy and a pizza party."

Charlie added, "For the last three years, Luther the tarantula in Ms. Sikes class has won. He's big, ugly, and the whole school loves him. Boogie has a secret weapon that will defeat that spider for sure."

"What's that?" asked the teacher.

"When Boogie hears music he starts to dance," said Allison.

"Allison, you're a genius," shouted Charlie.

"Finally, someone noticed," replied Allison.

Charlie hurried over to the CD player behind Mr. Beecher's desk and turned it on. He cranked the volume all the way up, and music flooded Room 7.

In a green flash, Boogie came out of the open top drawer of Mr. Beecher's desk. He climbed to the top of the desk, stood on his back legs, and began running in circles.

"He's dancing," laughed Ms. Phillips.

The class cheered as Boogie danced across the desk. When the song was over, Charlie turned off the CD player and Allison picked up the class pet.

"May I keep him at my desk for a little while?" asked Allison. "He's a little worked up, and I'm the only one who can calm him down. He sees me as a mother figure."

"That's because you look alike," joked Charlie.

"That's rude," snapped Allison. "You should apologize."

"You're right," said Charlie. "I apologize. Boogie, you're much cuter than Allison."

The class laughed as Allison stuck her tongue out at Charlie. He returned the favor.

"Put the lizard back in his cage," said Ms. Phillips.

"I'll do it," said Charlie. He reached for the lizard, but Allison refused to hand him over.

"He doesn't like you," insisted Allison. Charlie tried again, but Allison wouldn't budge. "Go away," she said. "You're bothering him."

"Give me the lizard," said Charlie as he grabbed Boogie's tail.

"Let go," said Allison.

"No," said Charlie as he pulled harder. That's when the end of Boogie's tail popped off. Allison let out a bloodcurdling scream and dropped the lizard. Charlie threw the tail in the air. The tail flew across the room and landed on Shelby's desk. She screamed and ran

to the front of the room. Soon, the entire class was screaming. The commotion was too much for Boogie. He scurried out the open door and raced down the hall.

Ms. Phillips covered the tail with a tissue. "Calm down. Boogie is not hurt," she explained. "Lizards can drop their tail when they feel threatened. Did anyone see where he went?"

"He ran into the hall," said Biff.

"Don't just stand here. Get that lizard!" shouted Ms. Phillips. The students of Room 7 stampeded into the hall, but Boogie had already disappeared.

Chapter 3
I Always Cry at Funerals

The students from Room 7 were still searching for the lost lizard when Dr. Brown spotted them in the hall. "What's all the commotion?" he asked.

The students all started talking at once. The principal held up his hand and they quieted down. "Back to class," ordered Dr. Brown. He followed the students into Room 7 where Ms. Phillips was standing next to the trash can.

"I found your class in the hall," said Dr. Brown. "They were causing quite a ruckus."

"I'm sorry," said Ms. Phillips. "They were looking for our class pet."

"Why is your pet in the hall?" asked the principal.

Charlie cringed. He was sure Ms. Phillips was about to tell the whole grisly tail story. Instead, Ms. Phillips said, "It's my fault. I let things get out of hand."

Dr. Brown let out a heavy sigh. "We can't have any more of these kinds of disturbances," he said. "Being a substitute teacher can be a tough job. Are you sure you're up to it?"

"I'll do better," said Ms. Phillips.

"I hope so," said Dr. Brown as he shuffled out the door.

"Where's Boogie's tail?" asked Shelby.

"I threw it away," said Ms. Phillips.

"Threw it away?" gasped Allison. "We can't just throw it away."

"We should have a funeral for it," suggested Shelby. "We could bury it in the flower bed by the flagpole."

Everyone got behind the idea quickly. When the first recess bell rang, the students lined up and slowly walked to the front of the school. Biff dug a hole and Charlie dropped the tail in and covered it with dirt.

Shelby began to cry and said, "Rest in peace."

"It's only a tail," said Biff.

"I know, but I always cry at funerals," said Shelby as she sniffed.

"Aren't we supposed to sing a sad song or have a speech?" asked Rhonda. "That's what they did at my uncle's funeral."

"Burying a tail is a lot different than burying a person," said Ms. Phillips. "Burying a tail is pretty strange."

"Uncle Harry was pretty strange, but we had a talk anyway," argued Rhonda.

"OK, does someone want to say a few words?"

asked Ms. Phillips.

Allison raised her hand, but before she could say anything, Biff put his hand over his heart and led everyone in the Pledge of Allegiance.

After the funeral, the students of Room 7 made lost lizard posters to hang in the halls. Allison's poster was a drawing of Boogie shaking his little fist and screaming, YOU HAVEN'T HEARD THE LAST OF THIS, CHARLIE BACON.

Charlie's poster was huge. LOST LIZARD. CAN DANCE. LIKES TO EAT FLIES. NICE PERSONALITY. PLEASE RETURN TO ROOM 7.

Biff's poster looked like an old west wanted poster. He drew a picture of Boogie wearing a cowboy hat and boots. Shelby used a bright pink marker to write on her poster. BOOGIE, PLEASE COME HOME. WE MISS YOU.

"You know Boogie can't read," said Charlie.

"Don't speak to me," replied Shelby. "This is your entire fault. You're the reason we don't have a pet to enter in the Classiest Pet Contest."

"I'm sure we'll find Boogie. These posters will do the trick," said Charlie.

During lunch recess, the students of Room 7 plastered their posters in the halls of Central Elementary. But by the end of the day, there was still no sign of Boogie.

Lost
Lizzard

Please
Return

WANTED
ALIVE
NOT DEAD

Boogie
Room 7
Our
Lizzard

Lost
Lizzard
can dance
to eat flies
personality
PLEASE

RETURN to
Room 7

Chapter 4

Life in the Jungle

"We should go talk to my brother, Zany," suggested Biff on the way home from school.

"Does he know a lot about lizards?" asked Charlie.

"He knows a lot about everything," said Biff. "He's in eighth grade."

Zany was in the backyard working on his cruiser bike when Charlie and Biff arrived. "What do you two numbskulls want?" asked Zany as he tightened a nut.

"That's a weird-looking seat," commented Charlie.

"It's a banana seat," said Zany. "They were popular when Dad was a kid. I'm making my bike retro."

"Cool," said Biff.

"It's not cool, it's groovy," said Zany. "Now go away so I can work."

"We need your help," said Biff.

"I lost our classroom pet. He's a lizard named Boogie," said Charlie. "We thought you might help us find him."

"You've come to the right man," said Zany, putting down the wrench. "I'll find your lizard for twenty dollars."

"I don't have that much money," said Charlie.

"How much do you have?" asked Zany.

"Zero," said Charlie. "I'm broke."

"Come back when you have some money," said Zany.

"We could help you work on your bike," offered Biff.

"Not interested," said Zany, grabbing a screwdriver.

"I don't want this thing to fall apart."

"That's what happened to Boogie," said Charlie.

"What does that mean?" asked Zany.

"Part of Boogie's tail fell off when Charlie grabbed him. That's why he ran away," explained Biff.

"I'll take the case if you give me the tail," blurted Zany.

"We already buried it," said Biff.

"Idiots," roared Zany. "Don't you know witches pay top dollar for lizard tails?"

Biff whispered to Charlie, "I told you he knew everything."

"What else do witches pay top dollar for?" asked Charlie.

"Bat toes, spider tongues, snake belly buttons," listed Zany.

"Slow down," said Charlie. "I want to write these

down." He pulled a pencil out of his backpack and picked up a sheet of bright yellow paper that was taped to the toolbox.

"Give me that," snapped Zany. "It has personal information on it."

Charlie read what was written on the paper, "Stay out of my toolbox. That means you, Zany. If you lose one more of my tools, I will ground you for life."

"Dad's going to be pretty upset when he finds out you were in his toolbox," said Biff.

Zany stood up and wiped his greasy hands on his jeans. "I've decided to take your cockamamie lizard case if you keep your yapper shut about the tools," he said.

"Deal," said Biff.

"Where did you last see Booger?" asked Zany.

"It's Boogie. We were at school," answered Charlie.

"We'll ride my cruiser to the scene," said Zany. "Climb on."

"I'm not getting on that thing without a helmet," insisted Charlie.

"Right," said Zany. He disappeared into the garage. He came out with an old football helmet and a construction worker hard hat. He handed them to Biff and Charlie. "These will protect what little brain matter you have."

Zany and Biff crammed onto the banana seat and Charlie sat on the handle bars. The wild, wobbly ride came to a stop at Central Elementary School.

"The front doors will be locked," said Charlie, jumping off the bike.

"If you were a lizard, would you stay in a lousy school if you didn't have to?" asked Zany. "Your lizard has busted out and he's not going back. He's headed for

the jungle."

"What jungle?" asked Biff.

"That jungle," said Zany, pointing at the jungle gym on the playground.

Zany marched to the jungle gym and got down on his belly. Charlie and Biff got down next to him. "The more we act like lizards, the sooner we find Boogie," said Zany.

Biff's brother went into full lizard mode. He flicked his tongue in and out and jerked his head side to side. "Think like a lizard," he whispered.

"What do they think about?" asked Charlie.

"If I were a lizard, I'd think about scaring girls," said Biff.

"You already scare girls," laughed Charlie.

"Idiots," said Zany. "Lizards think about eating. We find some flies and we'll find the lizard."

"There's always a bunch of flies buzzing around the flower bed where we buried Boogie's tail," suggested Charlie.

The boys crawled like three large lizards to the tulips. When they got close to the flowers, Charlie noticed that what he thought were flies were actually bees. "Watch out for the bees," he whispered.

The warning came too late. A bee landed on Zany's outstretched tongue. Suddenly, his eyes crossed and he screamed, "Da ee tung my unge!"

"Speak English," shouted Biff.

"I am eaking unglish," said Zany. "Da ee tung my unge!"

"I think a bee stung his tongue," said Charlie.

"Id a ee ing ur unge?" asked Biff in a loud voice.

"Idiots!" shouted Zany as he jumped on his cruiser and pedaled for home. Charlie and Biff kept looking

for Boogie. They hunted through the bushes. They searched the playground. They even scoured the garbage cans. There was no sign of Boogie.

"I don't think we're ever going to find him," said Biff. "He's danced out of our lives."

"I think you're right," said Charlie. "We're going to have to go to Plan B."

"What's Plan B?" asked Biff.

"I was hoping you knew," answered Charlie.

"The only Plan B that I know is when my mom burns dinner. She orders takeout food and calls it Plan B," said Biff.

"That's it," blurted Charlie.

"Good," said Biff. "I'm hungry."

"We're not buying food," explained Charlie. "We're going to buy a new lizard."

"How much do they cost?" asked Biff.

"That's what we're about to find out. Let's go to the pet store," said Charlie.

Chapter 5

Potty Mouth
Parrot

At Pat's Pet Palace the boys immediately went to a large green parrot near the front of the store. "Hello," squawked the bird.

"He can talk," said Biff.

"He can talk," repeated the bird. Both boys laughed.

"Biff's a weirdo," said Charlie.

"Biff's a weirdo," repeated the bird.

"Charlie has on dirty underwear," said Biff.

"Charlie has on dirty underwear," announced the bird. Both boys laughed harder.

"Can I help you?" asked a slender man wearing a Pat's Pet Palace shirt.

"We need a lizard," said Charlie.

"I just got a shipment in today," said the salesman leading the boys to the back of the store. "You can have any lizard in the terrarium for $24.95 plus tax."

"That's a lot of money," said Biff.

"Is there a discount if we don't take the whole lizard?" asked Charlie. "We don't really need the tail." The salesman looked confused.

"We're trying to replace our class pet," said Biff. "His tail fell off and he ran away. No one would notice if his replacement didn't have a tail."

"You need an inexpensive class pet," said the salesman, perking up. "I have lots of class pets that cost less than twenty-five dollars." The boys followed the salesman to a huge aquarium full of goldfish.

"Very cheap, very fun, and their tails won't fall off," said salesman with a huge grin. "I've sold a bunch of these to a first grade teacher the past few weeks."

Biff and Charlie stared at the tank of boring fish. "Are they trainable?" asked Biff. "Our lizard could dance."

"Afraid not," said the salesman.

"I think we're going to stick with the lizard," said Charlie. "I'll be back when I get the money."

"Sounds good," said the salesman.

"Where are you going to get that much money?" asked Biff.

"I'll think of something," said Charlie.

When Charlie got home, his mom's car was in the driveway. He burst through the front door and yelled, "Mom, where are you?"

"Hush down, you'll wake Jimmy," said Mrs. Bacon, hurrying into the living room. "I just got your little brother to sleep. If he doesn't get a nap, he's a real bear."

"A bear would be funner than a two-year-old," said Charlie.

"More fun," corrected Mom.

"I'm glad you agree," said Charlie. "Let's trade him to the zoo."

"Speaking of the zoo, it looks like wild animals have been living here. The house is a total disaster," said Mom. "How can you dirty every piece of clothing and dish in the house in just two days?"

"How was your weekend at Grandpa and Grandma's house?" asked Charlie, trying to change the subject.

"It was good to help Grandma for a couple of days, but I don't like coming home to a mess every time I go somewhere. There are going to be some changes made around here," said Mom.

"You could give me twenty-five dollars," suggested Charlie. "That would be a good change."

Charlie's mom laughed. "Does that mean yes?" asked Charlie.

"Oh, I'm sorry," said Mom. "Were you being serious? No, you can't have twenty-five dollars. Now go clean your room."

Charlie trudged to his room and closed the door.

His mom was right. His room was a disaster. He shoved the pile of dirty clothes with his foot and uncovered the family dog, Oscar.

"Big O, what are you doing here?" asked Charlie. "If you were a dancing lizard, you could solve my problem." The wiener dog wagged his tail and licked Charlie's hand.

Oscar came to live with the Bacon family when Great Aunt Wanda moved into Golden Vista Retirement Village. They adopted him because Golden Vista didn't allow pets.

Charlie's dad called Aunt Wanda, Wacky Wanda. He had nicknames for lots of their relatives. There was Dumb David, Loudmouth Reba, Lazy Larry, Pathetic Rick, just to name a few.

One time Charlie asked his dad why his nicknames sounded mean. "It's all in fun," explained Dad.

"They're fun names?" asked Charlie.

"Right," Dad said. "They're hilarious because they're true."

The next week the Bacon family was at a dinner celebrating Grandma's birthday. It was a dull party. Charlie thought if his dad would start calling people by their fun names, the party might pick up a little bit.

When Dad asked Uncle Rick to pass the beans, Charlie said, "You mean Pathetic Rick." When Dad asked Larry to pass the potatoes, Charlie chimed in with, "Don't you mean Lazy Larry?" When Dad thanked Reba for passing the rolls, Charlie said, "Loudmouth Reba, right, Dad?"

That's when Mom took Charlie in the hall to have a little chat. "I'm just using the names Dad calls them at home," Charlie said real loud. And then he started going through the list. When he said, "Wacky Wanda," a loud laugh erupted in the other room. Charlie and his mom hurried back into the dining room to find Aunt Wanda grasping a large wooden spoon and chasing Charlie's dad around the table. The family cheered when she trapped him in the corner. She made him apologize to the entire family.

Charlie's dad felt bad about the name calling so when Oscar needed a new home, he agreed to take him in. Charlie promised to take good care of Oscar, and Aunt Wanda promised to help him if he ever needed anything. Charlie decided it was time to cash in on that promise.

Chapter 6
Wacky Wanda

Charlie stopped at Golden Vista Retirement Village on his way home from school the next day. The director of Golden Vista escorted Charlie to the recreation room where he found Aunt Wanda playing pool with a chubby guy. He was pretty upset that Wanda was winning.

"Eight ball in the side pocket," said Wanda, looking down her pool stick.

When the black ball disappeared in the hole, the man stomped his foot and threw five dollars on the table. "Double or nothing," he said.

"Sorry," said Aunt Wanda, pocketing the five. "My

boyfriend's here."

"Watch her kid, or she'll get all your lunch money," said the large guy.

Aunt Wanda led Charlie down the hall to the cafeteria. "Let's get a snack and chat," she said. She opened a refrigerator and grabbed two bowls of lime Jell-O.

Charlie slurped a huge spoonful and got right to business. "I need a loan," he said.

"Don't we all?" said Aunt Wanda, sucking in a chunk of the wiggly dessert.

"I need to buy a pet," explained Charlie. "I lost our classroom pet and everyone's mad at me."

"When I taught school we didn't have animals in class, unless you count Robert Landers. That boy was hairy as a hamster," said Wanda with a laugh.

"We need a pet to enter in the Classiest Pet

Contest," added Charlie.

"What's that?" asked Wanda.

"It's a competition to see which class has the best classroom pet," explained Charlie.

"You mean like a beauty pageant for pets?" asked Wanda.

"Yeah, I guess," said Charlie.

"I remember my pageant days," said Aunt Wanda.

"You were in a beauty pageant?" asked Charlie.

"Bet your cheddar," said Wanda. "I was the Locket County Cheese Princess. You are in the presence of cheese royalty."

Charlie laughed and asked, "What does a cheese princess do?"

"I was a celebrity," said Wanda proudly. "I was in parades. I made appearances at fairs and festivals. If it was cheesy, I did it."

"Did you cut the cheese?" asked Charlie.

Great Aunt Wanda ignored Charlie's bad joke. "Being the Locket County Cheese Princess was one of the happiest years of my life," she said with pride.

"So you can see how much it means to our class to enter the contest," said Charlie.

"If it means that much to you, I'll do it!" announced Wanda.

"You'll loan me the money?" Charlie asked excitedly.

"Better than that, I'll be your class pet," said Aunt Wanda.

"You can't be a pet," insisted Charlie.

"Nonsense," said Wanda. "I'll be the best class pet you've ever seen. And I'll win that pageant too."

"Let's talk this over," said Charlie.

"No time for that, I've got plans to make," said Aunt

Wanda, shuffling Charlie out the door.

Charlie told his mom and dad about Great Aunt Wanda at dinner that night. "I told you that woman was wacky," said Dad. "She's totally flipped out this time."

"Aunt Wanda was a top teacher for over thirty years. I think she knows how to handle herself in a classroom," said Mom.

Charlie Bacon's tummy had butterflies as he headed to school the next morning. They weren't normal butterflies. These were evil, ninja butterflies doing battle in Charlie's stomach.

Great Aunt Wanda was waiting for him at the flagpole. She was wearing a fur coat even though it was a hot morning. "I thought I'd try to look the part," she said, rubbing the coat. "It's faux fur."

"What's a faux?" Charlie asked. "Is it like a wolf?"

"It means fake," she said.

"You're a fake class pet, wearing a fake fur coat. This is going to be real embarrassing," grumbled Charlie.

They entered through the front door of Central Elementary and stopped at the office. No one gets into Central Elementary without first checking in with Mrs. Simmons, the school secretary.

"What's up?" asked the secretary.

"I'm checking my Aunt Wanda in," said Charlie. "She's going to be a substitute today."

Mrs. Simmons looked surprised. "She's not on my list of subs," she said.

"Well, that's it. I guess we tried. You can't be the class pet," Charlie said, turning around.

"I'm helping out in Charlie's class," said Aunt Wanda in an official-sounding voice.

"Does Ms. Phillips know you're coming?" asked Mrs. Simmons.

"I've got a certificate of my teaching credentials if that will help," said Aunt Wanda. Mrs. Simmons looked at the paper.

"She thinks she's an animal," Charlie whispered to Mrs. Simmons. He thought this information would surely tip Mrs. Simmons off to Aunt Wanda's mental condition. The secretary ignored Charlie. She pulled out a visitor nametag and handed it to Aunt Wanda.

Charlie and Aunt Wanda meandered down the hall on the way to Room 7, as Charlie walked slower and slower. "I love the way a school smells," said Aunt Wanda.

"Then you'll love our room. It's the smelliest one in the building," said Charlie.

"Is that loud yelling coming from your room?"

asked Charlie's aunt.

"Since Mr. Beecher has been gone, we've become a pretty noisy bunch," said Charlie.

"That will be my first order of business," said Wanda.

"Wait a minute," said Charlie. "Your job is to stay in your cage and be quiet."

"We'll see about that," said Aunt Wanda as she marched into Room 7.

Charlie and Aunt Wanda made a beeline to Ms. Phillips. "This is my Aunt Wanda and she wants to be the new class pet," Charlie announced. "You can just tell her to go home and she'll leave."

Wanda shook Ms. Phillips' hand. "May I have a word in private?" asked Aunt Wanda.

"Of course," said Ms. Phillips, and they stepped out into the hall.

Charlie put his backpack away and sat down at his desk. "Is she really going to be the class pet?" asked Shelby. "She's s-o-o-o-o old."

"We'll probably have to mush up her food," said Lance.

"Where are we going to get a cage big enough for her?" asked Biff.

"I'm not changing the litter box," said Jordie.

Chapter 7

Let's Call Her Wrinkles

Ms. Phillips and Aunt Wanda came back in the room. That's when Charlie heard the words that he was sure would destroy his life. "This is Wanda and she's going to be helping in class for a while," said Ms. Phillips.

"Are you really the class pet?" asked Allison.

"Yes," answered Wanda. "I think I'm qualified for the position."

"You'll need a pet name," blurted Shelby. "How about Snowball?"

"What about Zippy?" asked Rayce.

"She's doesn't look very zippy," said Biff.

Jordie called out, "Let's call her Wrinkles. She's got lots of them."

"Wanda will do," said Charlie's aunt. "And from now on, there will be no calling out without raising your hand first."

"Pets can't make rules," said Allison. "It's a rule."

"You'll be surprised what this pet can do. Now, hush up," snapped Wanda.

"She's feisty," whispered Biff.

The door flew open and in charged Dr. Brown. Charlie sat up straight in his desk. He was sure the principal was going to kick his wacky aunt out of school.

"I heard you were in the building," said Dr. Brown.

"Hold it right there, Danny," said Aunt Wanda. "Let me get a good look at you."

Charlie couldn't believe his ears. His aunt had just

called Dr. Brown, Danny. "I've been waiting for this day," said Dr. Brown. Charlie's principal gave Aunt Wanda a huge hug. The entire class stared at Dr. Brown and Aunt Wanda embracing. It turned out that Aunt Wanda was Dr. Brown's fifth grade teacher.

"This wonderful lady is one of the reasons I decided to go into education," said Dr. Brown. "You'll learn a lot from her."

During morning announcements, Dr. Brown reminded everyone that their Classiest Pet reports needed to be finished by tomorrow. He then gave a special welcome to his former teacher.

Great Aunt Wanda didn't have to sit in a cage, which was a major disappointment to Charlie. She didn't even stay in her chair. When Jordie couldn't understand a math problem, Aunt Wanda was right there to help. During reading time, she made sure everyone kept up with the person who was reading out loud. She held Allison to one question at a time. When the students got too noisy, she'd pull a face that looked like a panther ready to pounce. The entire class would quiet down real fast.

Just before lunch, Allison raised her hand and asked, "Who's going to write the report for the Classiest Pet Contest? I'll be happy to do it."

"I think we should let Wanda pick the person for the job," said Ms. Phillips.

Charlie wasn't nervous about getting picked. He was sure Aunt Wanda already knew that he was a horrible writer. After she gave him an ugly green sweater last Christmas, Charlie's Mom made him write a thank-you note.

"Charlie will do a fine job," said Great Aunt Wanda. "He has a flare for the written word."

Dear Ant Wanda
    Thanks for the sweeter
Its pretty cool. I oxidently
left it in the cat box
and he oxidently used
it for a Toylet. Now
Mom won't let me
wear it.

            Love
              Charlie

"I don't want to," blurted Charlie. "I'm a terrible writer."

"You'll do a great job," said Aunt Wanda.

When the lunch bell rang, the students lined up at the door. "Thanks for ruining everyone's morning," said Rayce on the way to the cafeteria. "Your aunt is the worst pet in the world."

"I like her," chirped Allison. "She reminds me of what I'll be like when I'm a hundred years old. Of course, I won't have all those wrinkles."

"She scares me when she does that look," said Tony.

Charlie raced into the cafeteria. He grabbed a tray and hurried down the line to where his dad was serving grilled cheese sandwiches.

"How's your new class pet?" asked Chef Jeff.

"Horrible," said Charlie. "She's driving everyone nuts. She's ruining all the fun of having a substitute teacher."

Just then, Great Aunt Wanda walked into the cafeteria with Dr. Brown. The principal picked up two trays, and escorted Wanda to the front of the line.

"Hello, Jeff," said Wanda as she narrowed her eyes into a glare.

"Hello, Wanda," replied Dad, squinting like he was looking into a bright light. "Would you like a grilled cheese?"

"Did I ever tell you I was the Locket County Cheese Princess?" asked Wanda.

"Only a million times," said Dad.

"Part of my duties was to do TV commercials for the cheese commission. I still remember my lines," said Wanda, picking up a sandwich. She took a tiny bite and turned to an imaginary TV camera. "Cheese is always sure to please. It gives you strong bones and a happy tummy."

Dr. Brown applauded while Charlie's dad rolled his eyes. "We have a lot of students to serve," he said. "Please move along."

Dr. Brown and Aunt Wanda strolled to the teacher's lounge while Charlie sat down next to Biff. Charlie's best friend was devouring his cheese sandwich. "I've got to get your dad's recipe for this grilled cheese.

It's the tastiest sandwich in the world. What kind of cheese is this?"

"How should I know?" said Charlie. "All cheese is the same."

"That's not true," said Biff. "There's mozzarella, swiss, colby, spicy jack, mild cheddar, medium cheddar, and sharp cheddar. Sharp cheddar always gives me gas."

"Can you stop talking about cheese?" asked Charlie. "We've got a huge problem. Tomorrow morning, my aunt's going to stand next to me in front of the entire school while I tell everyone that she's our class pet."

"So?" said Biff.

"So I'm going to be the laughing stock of the school. This is the kind of weird story that goes viral on the Internet," argued Charlie.

"Then you'll be famous," said Biff, munching the last bit of his sandwich.

"Famous for all the wrong reasons," said Charlie. "I have to stop Aunt Wanda from being in that contest."

Chapter 8
Whirling Weiner Dog of Joy

After school, Charlie tried to get Aunt Wanda to go to Pat's Pet Palace. "It will be fun to look at all the animals," he said. "We could pick one out to be our new class pet."

"The only pet I want to see is my little Oscar," said Wanda. As they walked to Charlie's house, Aunt Wanda cracked Charlie up with her jokes.

"Why can't you be funny like this in class?" he asked.

"Laughing isn't a problem for your class," said Wanda. "They need synergy."

"Mom won't let me drink energy drinks," said

Charlie.

Great Aunt Wanda laughed and said, "Synergy isn't a drink. It's what happens when people work together."

Charlie opened the front door of his house for Aunt Wanda. "Oscar's probably in my room. I warn you, it's a little messy," he said. Aunt Wanda followed Charlie into his room.

"A tornado is a little messy compared to this," said Aunt Wanda. "This is a catastrophe."

"I like it this way," said Charlie.

Out of the mess came a whirling wiener dog of joy. Oscar spun in circles around Wanda's feet. "How's my baby?" asked Aunt Wanda, picking up the long dog. She gave him a kiss on the head and walked into the living room.

"I've got a fantastic idea," blurted Charlie. "Oscar can be our class pet. He'd love it."

"Absolutely not," insisted Aunt Wanda.

"Is that my favorite aunt's voice?" called Charlie's mom coming up from the basement. She gave Aunt Wanda a kiss on the cheek, and they both sat down on the couch.

While Charlie's mom and his aunt chatted, he trudged into his bedroom. He stepped over the dirty clothes, around the pile of toys, and plopped down on his unmade bed. He thought about writing the class pet report, but decided to take a nap instead.

The next morning, Aunt Wanda showed up at school wearing an elegant flamingo pink dress and long, snow-white gloves that came all the way up to her elbows. There was a huge white ribbon across her front that had Room 7 written in fancy cursive letters.

"I must admit I'm pretty excited. I haven't been in a pageant for many years," said Wanda. The bell rang and everyone but Tony took their seats. He was standing on his desk trying to look in the heating vent that was near the ceiling.

"Tony, take your seat," said Ms. Phillips.

Tony ignored her. "There's a monster in there," he said.

That brought Charlie and Biff to the top of their desks to get a look. Ms. Phillips got the flashlight out of the emergency kit and shined it into the vent. "I don't see anything," she said.

"It's there," argued Tony. "I can hear its claws scraping on the metal. It wants to kill us all."

The room fell silent as the students strained their ears to hear the monster. "This is nonsense," said Aunt Wanda. "Boys, get off of your desks."

Dr. Brown's voice came over the intercom and he read the morning announcements. "For the last item of business, don't forget the Classiest Pet Contest this morning. I'm looking forward to learning all about the animals of Central Elementary."

After the class recited the Pledge of Allegiance, Ms. Phillips asked Charlie if he'd like to rehearse his pet report in front of the class.

"I don't have one," mumbled Charlie.

Allison raised her hand. "I knew he'd flake out so I wrote an awesome report," she announced. She stood up and started reading from her notebook. "Wanda is our class pet. She's smart like an owl and has the eyes of an eagle. She's caring like a mother deer. She helps the kids who need help, which does not include me. She is the most fantastic pet in the universe."

"That's a fine speech," said Ms. Phillips. "Thank you, Allison."

"It won't do," said Wanda. "Charlie has to learn to be responsible. He'll give the report."

"But he'll embarrass the whole class," said Shelby.

"Can I just read Allison's speech?" asked Charlie. "It sounded pretty good."

"No," said Wanda. "You've got less than an hour. I suggest you start writing."

Chapter 9
Magical Bubbles

The school was buzzing, hissing, squawking, and tweeting as the classes filed into the gymnasium for the Classiest Pet assembly. Most of the pets were in cages on tables that lined the front of the multipurpose room. Some of the larger pets were on the floor. Wanda and Charlie were seated between the hamster twins from Mrs. Hardy's first grade class and Bob the turtle from Mr. Peterson's fifth grade class.

Dr. Brown quieted everyone down. "Welcome to Central Elementary Classiest Pet Contest. First, let's meet the judges. From Pat's Pet Planet we have Pat Jones. We have our custodian, Mr. Roy. Representing the teachers, we have Mr. Taylor and Mrs. Peterson. And finally, the student judges are Rosie Ford and Dante Woods. Now let's meet our contestants."

Mr. Long's class had a parakeet named Pete. A blond-haired girl with huge eyes stood next to the bird's cage and read her report. "This is Pete the parakeet. He's friendly and sometimes flies around the room. He has beautiful feathers and loves sunflower seeds. For his talent, he'll flap his wings." Pete fluttered his wings and there was a smattering of applause from the students.

Mrs. Miller's second grade class had an African pygmy hedgehog named Sylvia. A tall, skinny girl with brown hair read the report. "This is Sylvia. She's a hedgehog. She's super-duper cute. For her talent she'll eat a live mealworm." Sylvia chomped down the wiggling worm in two bites.

A chubby boy from Mrs. Streeter's third grade class stood up next. "This is Speedy. He's a hamster. He has a scientific name, but it's too long and hard to pronounce. He eats pellets and we give him apple slices for treats. For his talent he'll run in his exercise wheel." When Speedy refused to get in the wheel, the boy took a bow and sat down.

"This is Bob," mumbled a fourth grader from Mr. Dial's class. "He's a western box turtle. We feed him chopped-up veggies and sometimes a worm. We have to change his water every day because he gets confused and uses it for a toilet. It's pretty disgusting. Bob has a talent for playing peekaboo." The fourth grader yelled "Boo!" and Bob pulled his head and legs into his shell.

A first grader from Mr. Snyder's class stood up next and said, "This is Bubbles. She's a goldfish. She should be the classiest pet because she is magic. One time Max fed her the whole jar of fish food. The next day she was smaller and had a black spot on her tail. Another time Julie fed her glitter instead of fish food. The next day Bubbles was lots bigger and the black spot was gone. The day after Carter put her in his pocket for the entire recess, the black spot was back, only it was on the other side. Her talent is making bubbles."

Bubbles burped, and three bubbles floated to the top of the fishbowl. "Ta da!" sang out the first grader, holding out her arms. The whole school clapped long and loud for Bubbles.

It was silent when John from Mr. Reese's class got Luther out of his terrarium. The giant tarantula crawled up the fifth grader's arm. "Give it up for Luther," he yelled. The entire school started to cheer. "He's a brachypelma smithi which means he's super cool. He's from Mexico and can speak fluent Spanish. You know him. You love him. His talent is being totally awesome." The crowd gave another round of applause.

There were more hamsters, gerbils, and a colorful tree frog. Mr. Jones' class pet was a duck egg, which had no talent at all. Finally, Dr. Brown looked at Charlie and gave a nod. Charlie took center stage. Aunt Wanda stood next to him, smiling and waving to the audience.

"This is our class pet. Her name is Wanda," said Charlie.

Some kids started to laugh and a fourth grader called out, "She's not a pet. They're trying to cheat." Soon other students began heckling Charlie. "People can't compete against animals," shouted a fifth grader from Mr. Reese's class. "It's not fair."

The students' reaction was worse than Charlie had imagined. He whispered to Aunt Wanda, "Let's just sit down. This is too embarrassing."

"You can do it," said Aunt Wanda. She gave him an encouraging smile.

Dr. Brown silenced the crowd and Charlie began again. "This is my great aunt Wanda. She's not as fast as Speedy, or as strong as Bob the turtle. She doesn't eat worms like a hedgehog, or burp bubbles like a goldfish. But a hedgehog will never help you complete a math problem. A spider will never read you a book. And bubbles will never quiet the class down when they're getting out of control.

"These pets are here because they don't have a choice. They're kept in cages and pens. Aunt Wanda chose our class because we needed her help. That makes her the best class pet ever. And now for her

talent she's going to dance."

Biff turned on the CD player and Aunt Wanda started dancing. She boogied over to Dr. Brown and pulled him out onto the multipurpose room floor. Together they danced the "Boot Scootin' Boogie." The students and teachers all clapped to the beat. When the music stopped, Dr. Brown gave a grand bow, and Aunt Wanda curtsied. The entire school gave them a standing ovation.

Dr. Brown was still trying to catch his breath when he announced, "After a quick break, I'll read the judges' decision."

Aunt Wanda reached over, kissed Charlie on the forehead and said, "That was a wonderful speech. I'm very proud of you."

"That was a great dance," said Charlie. "I think you'll win."

Mr. Hansen, the P.E. teacher, entertained the students with some juggling while the judges tried to make up their minds. After several minutes, Dr. Brown stood back at the podium and said, "The decision is in, and it wasn't an easy one. All of the pets were fantastic. In fifth place, we have Pete the parakeet. Our fourth place winner is Sylvia from Mrs. Miller's class. Third place goes to Bob the western box turtle. The runner-up to the classiest pet is Luther the tarantula."

A gasp went through the multipurpose room. Someone had knocked the tarantula from his throne. Charlie was sure it was Great Aunt Wanda.

"Can I have a drumroll please?" asked Dr. Brown. The students began patting their legs to make their best drum sound. "The winner of the Classiest Pet Contest is Bubbles the magic goldfish. Mrs. Wright's class will receive the Classiest Pet Trophy and a pizza

party."

The first graders went nuts. They were jumping and shouting like maniacs. The students of Room 7 lined up and returned to class. They were all good sports about the decision, except for Aunt Wanda. She was not a good loser.

"I can't believe I lost a beauty pageant to an ugly fish," she snapped. "Did you see the eyes on that thing?"

"You lost to a turtle too," said Jordie.

"And a spider," added Shelby.

"Don't forget the hedgehog," said Biff laughing.

"Face it Aunt Wanda, you're a horrible pet," said Charlie.

"But a fantastic teacher," sang out Ms. Phillips. She started to clap and everyone joined in. The clapping woke up the monster in the vent.

"Heeeee's back," shouted Tony. This time everyone could hear the scratching.

Chapter 10

A Raccoon
with a Cold Sore

Ms. Phillips picked up the phone and called the office. "Mrs. Simmons, will you have the custodian bring his ladder to my room. There's a problem with the heating vent."

It didn't take Mr. Roy long to get to Room 7. He grumbled as he set up his ladder. "What's the problem?" he asked.

"There's a monster in the vent," blurted Tony.

"There are lots of monsters in this school. They're called students," said Mr. Roy, laughing.

As Mr. Roy started up the ladder, Dr. Brown came into the room. "I heard there's a problem with the ventilation system," he said.

"A monster," said Shelby in a spooky voice.

Mr. Roy took off the cover and looked in. "I don't see anything," he said. That's when Dr. Brown's cell phone started ringing. His ring tone was a popular country song. As the music played, the scratching grew louder.

"Now I see it," said Mr. Roy, scrambling down the ladder. "Whatever it is, it's in a hurry."

Just as Dr. Brown answered his phone, a green whirl tumbled out of the vent. It landed right on top of the principal's bald head. Dr. Brown froze in place. His eyes were shut tight.

"Boogie," the students yelled at the same time.

"Danny, stay calm," said Aunt Wanda.

Danny didn't stay calm. His loud, high-pitched scream sent Boogie scurrying to the floor. "I've got

to get back to the office," screeched the frightened principal as he sprinted out the door.

Allison picked up Boogie and cuddled him in her arms. "You've been a bad widdle lizard," she said in baby talk. Mr. Roy was still laughing as he fastened the vent cover back in place. He put the ladder under his arm and left.

Boogie's return had Room 7 buzzing. Lance and Tony got into a fight while getting the terrarium out of the closet. Shelby filled Boogie's water dish and bumped into Biff, causing water to splash on Rayce's head. Rayce yelled and shoved Jordie into Shelby who started to cry. Allison marched up to Ms. Phillips' desk and began tattling on everyone.

Charlie looked over at Aunt Wanda. He was waiting for her to give her panther stare, but she just stood there with her arms folded. That's when Ms.

Phillips brought out her own panther stare. It was more like a raccoon with a cold sore on its lip, but it worked.

Everyone quieted down real quick. Ms. Phillips took charge and gave everyone an assignment. Soon Boogie was safe in his terrarium and the students were sitting quietly in their seats.

"Wow," said Ms. Phillips. "How did you do that so quickly?"

Charlie raised his hand and said, "Synergy, Aunt Wanda told me about it." The students turned to look at Wanda, but her chair was empty. She was gone.

"Maybe she went to the bathroom," said Biff. "I heard old people have to go a lot."

"Her purse is gone too," said Allison. "I don't think she's coming back."

The synergy in Room 7 lasted for the rest of the

day. When Dr. Brown stopped by after lunch, the students were quietly working on thank-you cards for Aunt Wanda.

"I received a call from Mr. Beecher today," said Dr. Brown, beaming. "He named his son Daniel. He'll be away from the classroom for another couple of weeks. Can I count on this class to be responsible?"

"Everything is under control," said Ms. Phillips. "Thanks to a few tricks I learned from Wanda."

"Where is my former teacher?" asked Dr. Brown.

"She left this morning after Boogie came back. I think she retired from the classroom pet business," said Ms. Phillips.

"Charlie, stop by my office on your way home today," said Dr. Brown. "I have something for your aunt."

Charlie hurried to Golden Vista Retirement Village

as soon as school was over. He found Aunt Wanda playing pool in the recreation room. "Why did you leave without saying good-bye?" he asked.

"Your pet came home and Ms. Phillips had things under control," said Aunt Wanda. "Your class didn't need me anymore."

"We made these thank-you cards for you. Mine's the best," said Charlie.

"Wonderful," said Aunt Wanda, taking the cards. "I really enjoyed being back in the classroom for a couple of days. It reminded me of how much I loved teaching."

Charlie pulled an envelope out of his backpack. "When Danny, I mean Dr. Brown, found out you'd left, he gave me this letter to give to you," said Charlie.

When she read the letter, Wanda's face blossomed into a smile. "What does it say?" asked Charlie.

"It seems that Speedy the hamster has disappeared," said Wanda. "There's a classroom pet job available if I'm interested."

"I wouldn't take it," said Charlie. "Mrs. Streeter's class is the rowdiest in the school."

Aunt Wanda was still smiling when she put the letter and thank-you cards in her purse. "How about a game of pool?" she asked.

"I can't," said Charlie. "I'm going to clean my room. I want to surprise Mom. Do you think it's possible to teach Oscar about synergy? I could use some help."

Great Aunt Wanda took Charlie by the arm and said, "Let's go find out."

About the Author

Gary Hogg is the author of more than twenty books. His hilarious stories include *Look What the Cat Dragged In, I Heard of a Nerd Bird*, and the popular *Spencer's Adventures* series. Gary says his fourth grade teacher inspired him to put his wild ideas into stories instead of acting them out in class. She kept her sanity and he became a writer. Of all the characters he's created, Gary says Charlie Bacon is the most like him.

Gary is a popular speaker and guest author. He has inspired over 2 million students to be better writers with his popular *Writing is Exciting!* assembly and workshop program. You can learn about him at **www.garyhoggbooks.com**.